Doctor Dolittle's Ambulance

Red Fox Read Alone

Red Fox Read Alones are fab first readers! With funny stories and cool illustrations, reading's never been so much fun!

- **Doctor Dolittle's First Adventure**
  Hugh Lofting, illustrated by Sarah Wimperis
- **Doctor Dolittle and the Lighthouse**
  Hugh Lofting, illustrated by Sarah Wimperis
- **Doctor Dolittle Takes Charge**
  Hugh Lofting, illustrated by Sarah Wimperis
- **Tiger Boy**
  Chloë Rayban, illustrated by John Prater
- **Jamie and the Whippersnapper**
  Enid Richemont, illustratred by Graham Smith
- **Cat's Witch and the Monster**
  Kara May, illustrated by Doffy Weir
- **Eric and the Wishing Stone**
  Barbara Mitchellhill, illustrated by Bridget Mackeith
- **Davy and Snake**
  Amanda McCardie, illustrated by Sue Heap

Based on the stories by

HUGH LOFTING

Retold by Charlie Sheppard

Doctor Dolittle's Ambulance

Illustrated by Sarah Wimperis

RED FOX

A Red Fox Book

Published by Random House Children's Books
20 Vauxhall Bridge Road, London SW1V 2SA

A division of The Random House Group Ltd
London Melbourne Sydney Auckland
Johannesburg and agencies throughout the world

1 3 5 7 9 10 8 6 4 2

This Read Alone Novel first published in Great Britain
by Red Fox 2000

Printed and bound in Denmark by
Nørhaven A/S, Viborg

Papers used by Random House Group Ltd are natural,
recyclable products made from wood grown in sustainable forests.
The manufacturing processes conform to the
environmental regulations of the country of origins.

The Random House Group Limited Reg. No. 954009

www.randomhouse.co.uk

ISBN 0 09 940701 9

Contents

A Very Unusual Doctor

Once upon a time in the little town of Puddleby-on-the-Marsh there lived a doctor, and his name was John Dolittle. He was an ordinary looking man, a little on the plump side, and he lived in an ordinary looking house, a little on the big side, but he wasn't an ordinary sort of doctor.

You see, he didn't give out pills and medicines to sick people. No, Doctor Dolittle was an animal doctor and he gave out pills and medicines to sick animals. But even more extraordinary, he was the only animal doctor in the world who could actually speak animal languages.

You can imagine how much the animals liked that. A doctor who could bark in dog language and cheep in bird language. A doctor who could ask animals what was the matter with them instead of just scratching his head in a puzzled sort of way. A doctor who loved animals more than people.

In fact because Doctor Dolittle loved animals so much, he kept all sorts of pets. Besides the goldfish in the pond at the bottom of his garden, he had rabbits in the pantry, white mice in his piano, a squirrel in the linen closet, and a hedgehog in the cellar. He had a cow with a calf, an old lame horse, chickens and pigeons, two lambs and many other animals.

But his favourite pets were Jip the Dog; Dab-Dab the duck; Chee-Chee the monkey; Gub-Gub the pig; Polynesia the parrot; and the owl Too-Too.

Before long all the animals in Puddleby wanted to be treated by the wonderful doctor. Soon they'd told their friends about John Dolittle, and those friends had told their friends, so that one day Doctor Dolittle looked out of his window and saw a line of animal patients stretching twice round the garden and out the front gate.

'Oh, dear,' he said to himself, 'I really think it's time I got someone to help me.'

A New Assistant

Now the animals who lived with the Doctor were already very helpful around the house. Dab-Dab the duck dusted and made the beds; Jip the dog swept the floors; Chee-Chee the monkey did the mending; the owl Too-Too was in charge of the money; and the pig Gub-Gub did the gardening. Polynesia the parrot was the housekeeper because she was the oldest.

But Doctor Dolittle needed some help in the surgery and so he decided to ask Tommy Stubbins to be his assistant.

Tommy was the cobbler's son and he was nine and a half when he first met Doctor Dolittle. Tommy loved animals almost as much as the Doctor did. His parents were very poor, too poor to send him to school, so he spent most of his time in the fields looking after wild creatures.

Well, when he heard about a doctor who could actually talk to animals, Tommy wanted to help him more than anything in the world. And when Doctor Dolittle heard how much Tommy loved and cared for animals, he decided to make him his assistant. So Tommy's parents agreed that their son could live at the Doctor's house and help with odd jobs around the place. In return the Doctor agreed to teach Tommy to read and write, and to talk to the animals!

Tommy loved living with the Doctor and his animal family. Every morning he helped Chee-Chee to make breakfast for the Doctor. When all the dishes were put away, he cleaned the surgery, rolled the bandages and fed the animals.

Once his jobs were done, he would go into the Doctor's study and begin his lessons in animal languages. It wasn't long before he could talk to all the animals and the Doctor was very pleased to have such a clever assistant.

In the evenings Tommy helped the Doctor in the surgery. He learned to dress cuts and scratches, and give out the correct amounts of medicine.

And when he went into Puddleby to collect things for the Doctor he would carry his head very high. Little boys who had laughed at him before because he was too poor to go to school, now pointed him out to their friends and whispered, 'You see him? He's a doctor's assistant. And he's not even ten years old yet.'

A Helping Hand

Doctor Dolittle found life much easier now that he had some help, and soon the queue of animals wanting to see him stretched only as far as the front door. Cats with sore tummies, birds with broken wings, squirrels with bumped heads – Doctor Dolittle cured them all.

One week, however, the Doctor had lots of serious cases of hurt dogs. Dogs run over by carts, dogs kicked by horses, sick and homeless strays. By the time some of these dogs got to the surgery they were so badly hurt that the Doctor had a hard time pulling them through.

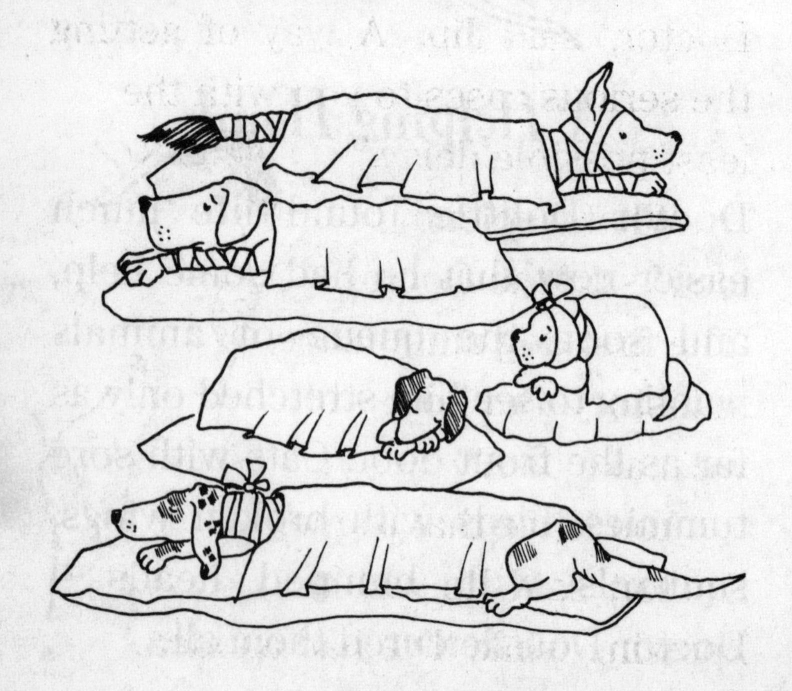

'If only I could see them sooner,' he said. 'It takes so long for them to limp all the way to the house or for Tommy to carry them here from Puddleby. They're usually really very sick indeed by the time I begin to treat them.'

'We need a dog ambulance, Doctor,' said Jip. 'A way of getting the serious cases to you with the least possible delay.'

'What a splendid idea,' said the Doctor. 'The first dog ambulance in history. But how will we make one?'

'You leave that to me, Doctor,' said Jip with a knowing wink. 'I've had an idea.'

Building the Ambulance

'Tommy,' said Jip at breakfast the next day. 'I need your help. We've got to have a dog ambulance.'

'A dog what?' said Tommy, choking on his porridge.

'An ambulance,' Jip repeated. 'I've already spoken to the Doctor about it and he thinks it's a good idea.

At the end of the road there are a couple of mongrel greyhounds. They're kind of funny to look at, but they're very speedy. They have already agreed to take turns pulling the ambulance. So we will have no difficulty with that part of it. What we need is the ambulance carriage itself and a harness for the greyhounds. Do you think you could build us a carriage and get your father to make us a harness?'

'Well, Jip,' said Tommy, 'I don't know. But I am quite willing to try.'

So that same evening Tommy went over to the Stubbins' cobbler shop to look for his father. Mr Stubbins was very busy but when he heard what his son wanted he agreed to make the harness in his spare time.

'And take this cake back to the good Doctor,' said Mrs Stubbins as Tommy kissed his parents good-bye. 'Tell him we're very pleased with your reading and writing.'

When he got back to the house, Tommy, who prided himself on being something of a mechanic, started to make the carriage.

Using a pair of pram wheels,

some pieces of wood,

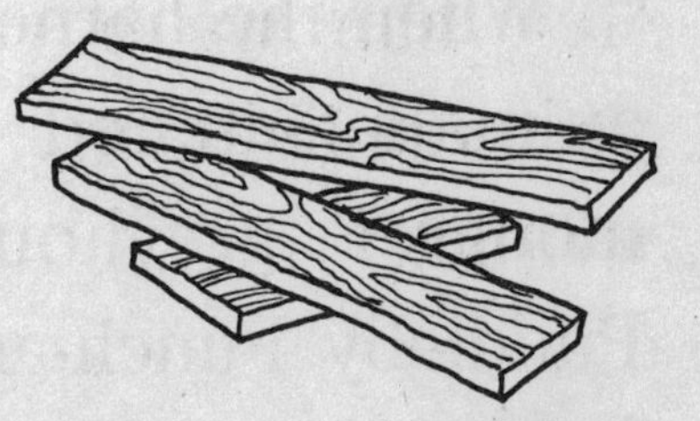

and a few springs out of an old bed 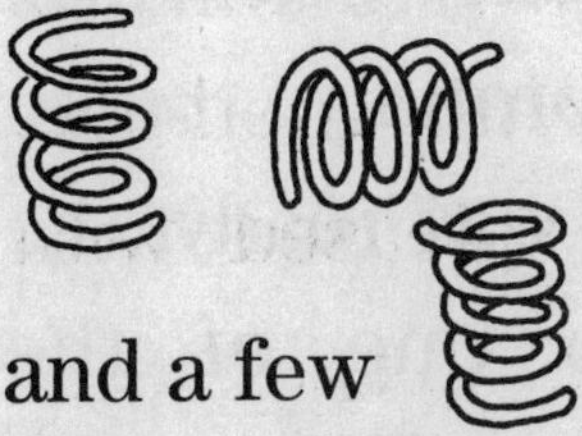 he built a very decent looking runabout, light enough to be pulled by a dog. He and Chee-Chee painted it white and put a Red Cross flag on it and a bell. It really was a super little ambulance.

'Oh my,' said Dab-Dab, as she waddled into the garden. 'That's quite something, Tommy Stubbins.' And Tommy grinned proudly.

When the harness was ready, the animals hitched up one of the mongrel greyhounds. Toby, the Puddleby Punch-and-Judy dog, was called over to help out. Toby had agreed to be the ambulance nurse and he rushed over to see the wonderful new carriage.

'Jump up,' shouted Jip. So Toby hopped onto the back and Jip, as the ambulance surgeon, drove around the garden at twenty miles-an-hour – much to the astonishment of Polynesia and Gub-Gub who were watching from the window.

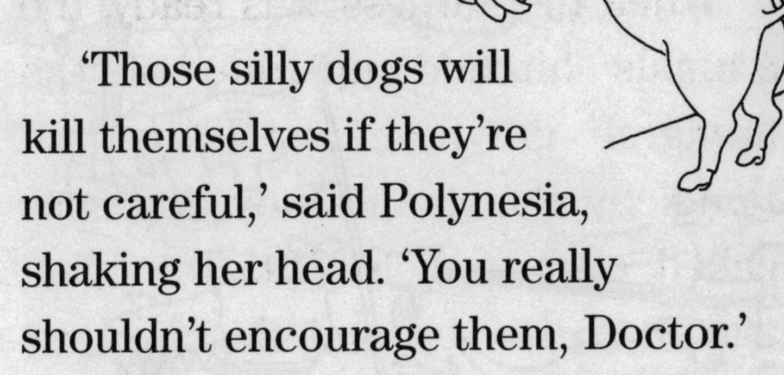

'Those silly dogs will kill themselves if they're not careful,' said Polynesia, shaking her head. 'You really shouldn't encourage them, Doctor.'

'Oh, don't fuss,' said Doctor Dolittle. 'I think their ambulance is going to be very useful. Very useful indeed.'

Emergency!

Doctor Dolittle, Tommy Stubbins and the animals were very proud of the new Dog Ambulance. Night and day, from then on, one of the greyhounds was kept harnessed up ready to answer emergency calls.

'This will help Doctor Dolittle a lot, Tommy,' said Jip. 'I just hope we don't get so many cases that we can't help everybody.'

In actual fact, quite the opposite happened. As soon as there was a brand-new Dog Ambulance ready for all emergencies, all dog casualties suddenly seemed to have stopped. The greyhounds stood in the harness from morning to night but no one needed their help.

Jip was very disappointed. Finally he became so desperate to try out the new ambulance that he and Toby decided secretly between them that if no case came along soon they would have to make one.

After many days of waiting they proudly (without telling the Doctor) led their ambulance out through the streets of Puddleby on their own. They did this partly because they wanted everyone to see the fine vehicle in all its glory, and partly because they hoped to find a 'case' by chance to try it out on.

While they were parading through the town they came upon Gub-Gub, the Doctor's pet pig. He was in a back street sitting on a rubbish heap.

Gub-Gub loved to explore rubbish heaps and he often found tasty things to eat in them. On this occasion the poor pig had eaten some bad turnips and was looking rather green in the face from a slight stomach ache.

'Are you all right?' asked Toby.

'Not really,' said Gub-Gub. 'My tummy hurts so I think I'll lie down here for a while. Please tell the Doctor I'll be back after I've had a little sleep.'

‘Ah! A serious case!’ cried Jip, rushing the ambulance up alongside the rubbish heap. ‘We must get you back to the surgery as quickly as possible, Gub-Gub.’

Then Nurse Toby, under the direction of Surgeon Jip, pounced upon poor Gub-Gub and began dragging him onto the ambulance.

They would have preferred a dog patient to try their new equipment on, but a pig was better than nothing.

'Leave me alone!' bawled Gub-Gub, kicking out in all directions. 'I've only got a stomach ache. I don't want to go on your ambulance!'

'Don't listen to him,' ordered Jip. 'He's delirious. Appendicitis most likely. It's a rush case, Nurse Toby. We must get him home quick!'

The two of them rolled Gub-Gub's fat body onto the ambulance. Jip sprang onto the driver's seat while Toby sat on the 'delirious' patient to hold him down.

Like a bullet from a gun the greyhound bounded away at full speed towards the Doctor's home.

Meanwhile Jip clanged the bell loudly to clear the road ahead and drown the shouts of the first patient to use the Dog Ambulance.

Look Out!

It was an unforgettable ride – for the staff of the ambulance, for the people of Puddleby who watched in amazement and, most of all, for the patient.

With its clanging bell, the strange ambulance streaked up the High Street. A policeman ordered it to stop but the greyhound took no notice. He was determined to get the sick pig back to Doctor Dolittle as quickly as possible. Gaining speed at the bottom of the hill, the ambulance shot round a corner on two wheels, scattering scared people left and right.

'Faster, faster!' shouted Jip to the greyhound. Poor Gub-Gub shut his eyes and squealed even louder.

'Look out!' shouted Toby suddenly as the ambulance got closer to Kingsbridge. Here the road narrowed as it crossed the river, and standing in the middle of the path was a wheelbarrow. The greyhound was going too fast to stop so he tried to swerve instead.

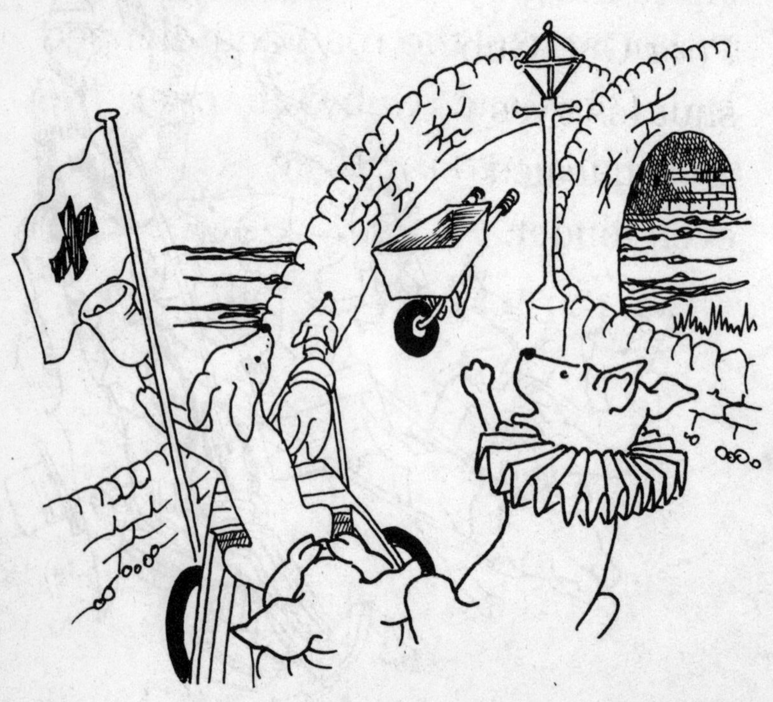

With Gub-Gub's extra weight added to that of the two dogs, the springs of the ambulance were under a lot of strain. The hub of the right back wheel only just touched the lamppost. But it was enough to throw the over-loaded, wobbling carriage off balance. On one wheel, it shot across the road and dumped Jip, Toby and Gub-Gub over the bridge and into the river.

Mud Bath

Luckily, the river was at a low tide so there were wide stretches of black mud next to the water. Poor Gub-Gub couldn't swim and if the river had been full he would not have been able to make it to the side.

Jip and Toby, on the other hand, *could* swim and would have much preferred a clean river to the dirty mud that was waiting for them below the bridge. All three landed with an oozy splash.

It broke the fall nicely, but the animals were now black from head to foot. The dogs didn't forget that they had a patient to look after, though. They tried to dig the struggling, squealing pig out of his mud bath.

'Get off me,' shouted Gub-Gub. But the poor pig, who was fatter than the dogs, had sunk deep into the mud and couldn't get out on his own.

At last the dogs managed to drag the squeaking pig onto firmer ground. 'Don't worry, Gub-Gub,' said Jip. 'We'll look after you.'

'That's what I'm afraid of,' said the frightened pig. He may not have been a proper case for the ambulance when he was carried off the rubbish heap, but by the time they had got him out of the mud, Gub-Gub really was in need of some attention.

A New Patient

Back on the bridge, the dogs were now completely clothed in a new uniform of black mud. They rolled the patient back onto the ambulance, jumped in after him and went away as fast as ever. In fact, they went even quicker this time. A big crowd had gathered at the bridge and the dogs were afraid that a policeman might appear at any moment and stop them.

For about a mile all went well. But as they turned into Oxenthorpe Road at full gallop, they had another accident. A handsome, overfed poodle was crossing the road with his nose in the air.

Suddenly, seeing the ambulance coming towards him at twenty-five miles-an-hour, he lost what little wits he had, ran first this way and then that and finally ended up under its wheels.

The carriage did not entirely capsize, but it tipped up enough as it went over him to throw poor Gub-Gub out again – this time into the gutter. The fiery greyhound was brought to a standstill and Jip ran back to take charge of the situation.

Gub-Gub was lying on his back in the gutter, yelling blue murder, his legs waving in the air. In the middle of the road the fat poodle was also lying on his back and howling, mostly with anger and fright. Surgeon Jip and Nurse Toby held a quick meeting.

'What shall we do?' asked Toby. 'The ambulance isn't big enough for both patients.'

'Our first duty is to the original patient,' said Jip. 'We must take Gub-Gub and come back for the poodle.'

'But this is supposed to be a *Dog* Ambulance,' argued Toby. 'Gub-Gub isn't even a dog. I think we should take the poodle and come back for the pig.'

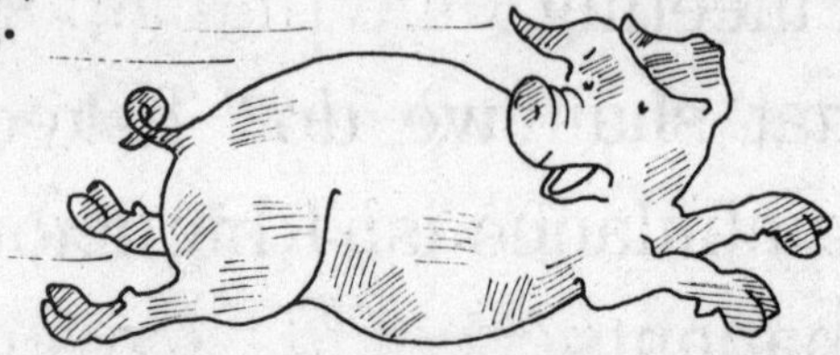

But while this discussion was going on, Gub-Gub, afraid that he might be forced to get back into the ambulance, suddenly sprang up and ran away as fast as he could. Sore as he was from his fall and his stomach ache, he had had enough of Jip's first aid.

This solved the problem for the staff of the Dog Ambulance very nicely. Jip grabbed the poodle by the scruff of the neck and dumped him into the ambulance, sprang in once more and gave the word to go.

It wasn't until the ambulance had done another mile that Jip suddenly realized he had left Toby behind. But the Punch-and-Judy dog, running as fast as he could, arrived at the surgery on foot, minutes behind the ambulance.

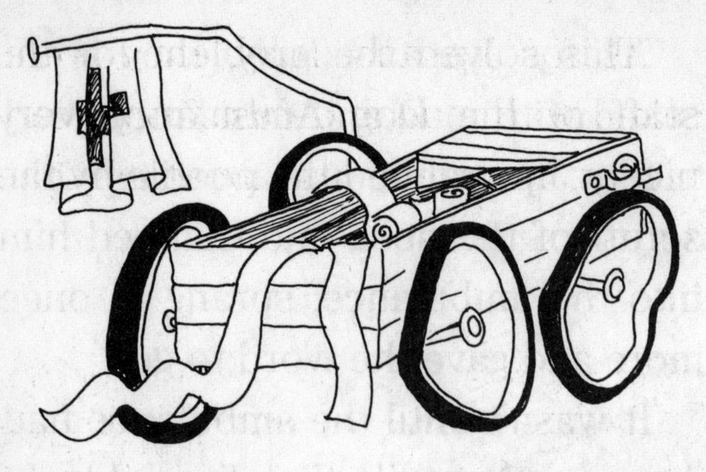

Home at Last

By the time the Dog Ambulance reached the surgery, it had certainly lost much of its original smartness. The wheels were bent and wobbly, the bell holder was twisted up like a corkscrew and the bell had gone. The first-aid box beneath the driver's seat had burst open and bandages were trailing from it in the dust of the road behind.

As for Jip and Toby, they were caked with mud and dust from head to foot. You could just about tell that they were dogs.

'What on earth's going on?' asked Doctor Dolittle as the ambulance came to a noisy halt outside the door and a very angry poodle jumped off the stretcher.

'I'll tell you what's going on, Doctor Dolittle!' shouted the poodle who recognised the great doctor at once. 'First of all I was run over by these crazy dogs in this killing machine. And as if that wasn't enough, they then decided to kidnap me outside my own gate. I was only going for a walk and now I'm black and blue all over and miles from home.'

Just as the poodle had finished speaking, his mistress, who had followed the ambulance in a cab, appeared in the front garden and also began shouting at the Doctor.

'I've heard all about you, Doctor Dolittle,' she shouted. 'You and your crazy wild animals. But I really think things have gone too far when a man trains a gang of dogs to kidnap and steal other dogs. I will be talking to the police about this, you see if I won't.'

The Doctor was just getting ready to answer her when Gub-Gub arrived, howling like a lost child who has been punished for something he didn't do. He began to tell the Doctor about the wicked deeds of the Red Cross Brigade who had carried him off against his will, thrown him over a bridge into the river, then rushed him over a bumpy street for a few more miles and finally tipped him out into the gutter.

By the end of these angry speeches, Jip and Toby were beginning to feel that their services had not been appreciated.

'I'm terribly sorry,' said Doctor Dolittle to the poodle owner. 'I'm sure the dogs meant well and I certainly didn't give them permission to go charging around Puddleby causing so much trouble. Let me have a look at your dog. Perhaps I can bandage him up.'

Doctor Dolittle shot an angry look at Jip and went into the house.

The poodle owner followed him, mumbling as she went. Gub-Gub limped in behind them leaving a trail of mud on the carpet, which Dab-Dab looked at in horror.

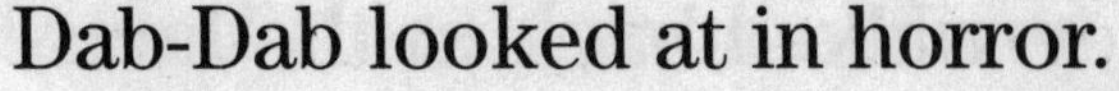

Outside, Tommy undid the greyhound's harness and separated him from the ambulance. The poor dog was exhausted and he slunk away home. As for Jip and Toby, they decided not to follow the Doctor and explain what had happened. They went miserably down to the fishpond and washed the mud off themselves. They didn't say a word until they walked back to the house for supper. Then Jip broke the silence and said, 'We shouldn't have started with that ridiculous pig. He always makes a mess of everything.'

In the meantime, the poodle and his mistress had left. Doctor Dolittle had managed to cheer them both up and persuade them not to go to the police about the ambulance. As Jip and Toby came into the kitchen, Gub-Gub was still sulking by the fire.

'Well,' said the Doctor. 'You dogs have certainly had an adventure. I know you meant well but I think from now on we'll let Tommy Stubbins collect the dog casualties, don't you?'

'Yes, Doctor,' they said, their heads bowed.

'Now come and eat your supper and let's hear no more of this Dog Ambulance,' said the Doctor.

Jip and Toby agreed and sat up at the table. They were very hungry after such a busy afternoon. Chee-Chee put a jug of milk on the table and brought a large steaming pie out of the oven.

'What's in that?' asked Gub-Gub, licking his lips and forgetting he was supposed to be sulking.

Jip sniggered. 'Turnip,' he said, with a cheeky grin. 'Big bad turnips followed by mud pudding.'

Gub-Gub turned rather pale. 'Suddenly I don't feel very hungry,' he said.

And the Doctor threw back his head and began to laugh.

RED FOX READ ALONE

Based on the stories by

HUGH LOFTING

Doctor Dolittle

IT TAKES A SPECIAL BOOK TO BE A RED FOX READ ALONE!

Doctor Dolittle's First Adventure

Doctor Dolittle and the Lighthouse

Doctor Dolittle's Ambulance

Doctor Dolittle Takes Charge